This book belongs to

....

CREDITS

Narrator	CINDY ROBINSON
Terence	JESSE MCCARTNEY
Tinker Bell	MAE WHITMAN
Vidia	PAMELA ADLON
Lizzy	LAUREN MOTE
Dr Griffiths	MICHAEL SHEEN
Fawn	ANGELA BARTYS
Clank	JEFF BENNETT
Bobble	ROB PAULSEN
The Driver	JEFF BENNETT
Rosetta	KRISTIN CHENOWETH

Read-Along Story Produced by TED KRYCZKO and JEFF SHERIDAN
Mastered by JEFF SHERIDAN
Assistant Engineer: FRANK TRUBÉ
Adapted by LEIGH STEPHENS

℗ 2010 Walt Disney Records.
© 2011 Disney Enterprises, Inc.

First published by Parragon in 2011

Parragon
Queen Street House
4 Queen Street
Bath BA1 1HE, UK

Materials and characters from the movie
Tinker Bell and the Great Fairy Rescue
Copyright © 2011 Disney Enterprises, Inc.
Visit www.DisneyFairies.com

The fairies of Pixie Hollow have been told to stay far away from humans. But when Tinker Bell is captured by a little girl, her friends have to work together to rescue her. To find out what happens, read along with me in your book. You will know it is time to turn the page when you hear this sound. . . .

Let's begin now.

Bath • New York • Singapore • Hong Kong • Cologne • Delhi
Melbourne • Amsterdam • Johannesburg • Auckland • Shenzhen

*T*inker Bell and the fairies of Pixie Hollow soared through the sky. They were on their way to bring summer to the mainland.

Summer was the fairies' busiest season. They would be staying on the mainland for a few months to get all their work done.

Tinker Bell's friend Terence flew up next to her on a white dove. "Hey, Tink! You ready for your first summer on the mainland?"

"Absolutely! It's so beautiful out here. I can't believe we get to stay for the whole season!" Tinker Bell had never been so excited.

"Well, what are we waiting for? Race you down!"

Tink and Terence landed in a clearing. "Come on, Tink, let's
go inside!"

Tinker Bell looked around. "Inside?"

"Tink, fairy camp isn't out here in the open. We need to stay hidden
from the humans."

Terence walked over to an old oak tree and pulled back a cluster of
leaves. There, beneath the tree, was a camp bustling with fairies. One
fairy was teaching crickets to sing. Another painted stripes on a group
of bumblebees, while a third painted pretty designs on butterflies'
wings. Everyone looked very busy!

Tinker Bell couldn't wait to start tinkering!

Terence, a dust talent, had to go deliver pixie dust to all the fairies in the camp. "Tink, don't worry. You'll find something to fix."

"I hope so. In the meantime, I need to go find some lost things."

Tinker Bell was on her way out when Vidia, a fast-flying fairy, flew right into her path. "You're not going near the human house, are you?"

Tink's eyes grew wide with excitement. "There's a human house?"

Suddenly, a loud CRACK echoed through the camp. All the fairies were startled. Fawn splattered paint on a butterfly's wing before it flew off. Other fairies hid under leaves or between flowers.

But Tinker Bell wanted to know where the noise had come from. She flew high above the tree and saw a car on the road. Fascinated, she chased after it.

"Tinker Bell!" Vidia took off after her.

Tinker Bell followed the car until it stopped at a house in the country.

A little girl named Lizzy got out with her father, Dr Griffiths, and their cat, Mr Twitches.

"Thank goodness we're here, Father! It's just like I remember it."

"Well, of course, my darling."

Tinker Bell watched from a nearby tree as the family went into the house. Then she flew up to the car for a closer look.

"Vidia, this is amazing! It's a carriage that moves by itself. There's no horse!" Tinker Bell zipped into the engine.

Vidia hovered nervously outside.

"I don't care, Tinker Bell. You shouldn't be this close to the human house!"

But Tink wasn't listening. She had found an interesting lever and she just had to pull it. "Let me know if this does anything!"

Suddenly, Vidia was sprayed with a stream of water. She was still in shock when Tinker Bell flew out of the engine. "Vidia, you're all wet."

Vidia glared at Tink. "You don't say."

Just then, Lizzy and her father returned to unload the car. Tink and Vidia froze.

While they watched the humans, a butterfly fluttered around. It was the one Fawn had splattered with paint when the car had driven past the fairy camp.

Dr Griffiths stopped unloading the luggage to take a look. "The wings have two entirely different patterns. Why, that's nearly impossible!"

"Well, I guess that's just the way the fairies decided to paint it."

"Lizzy, fairies do not paint butterfly wings because, as you know, fairies are not real." Dr Griffiths grabbed his journal and began sketching the butterfly.

Lizzy didn't believe her father. She knew fairies were real. She had even made a fairy house to catch one in. She was going to take it to the meadow and she wanted her father to go with her.

But Dr Griffiths was too busy. "Not now, Lizzy, I have to update my field journal. My interview at the museum is tomorrow night."

Dr Griffiths followed the butterfly. Lizzy skipped off in the other direction.

When the coast was clear, Tinker Bell and Vidia came out from under the car. Vidia couldn't fly because her wings were still wet. Tink offered to walk back to fairy camp with her.

As they crossed the meadow, Tink spotted a trail of buttons. "Wow! These will be perfect for the new wagon prototype I've been working on." She began to stack them in her arms. She wanted Vidia to help, too.

"Tinker Bell, I am not carrying this human junk back to camp." Suddenly, Vidia stopped in her tracks. The buttons led right to Lizzy's fairy house!

Tinker Bell wanted to explore. But Vidia wanted to leave right away. "Let's go!"

"Tinker Bell, we're not supposed to go near human houses!"

"Oh, come on, Vidia. It's perfectly safe." Tink hopped over the buttons leading to the door. Then she went inside.

The fairy house was filled with human objects. Tink began to fiddle with an old pocket watch that hung on the wall.

"Oh, really?" Vidia decided it was time to teach Tinker Bell a lesson.

With a wave of her arms, Vidia whipped up a gust of wind. The door to the fairy house slammed shut while Tinker Bell was still inside.

"Huh, not so safe now, is it?" Vidia hoped she had scared Tink enough to make her come out and head back to fairy camp.

Suddenly, Vidia heard a twig snap. Someone was coming! She tugged on the door to let Tink out, but it wouldn't budge. "Tink, someone's coming!
The door is stuck!"

Tinker Bell thought Vidia was still trying to trick her. "Oh, come on, Vidia. You can do better than that."

Vidia jumped behind some plants as Lizzy walked up to the fairy house.

Inside, Tinker Bell noticed that Vidia had gotten very quiet. "Vidia? Vidia?" She tried to open the door and discovered that it really was stuck.

Suddenly, Tink looked up and saw a giant eye staring at her through the window!

Lizzy couldn't believe what she was seeing. "A fairy . . . it's a real fairy!" Lizzy picked up the fairy house and took off down the path.

Vidia watched in horror from her spot behind the plants. "Oh, no . . . what have I done?"

Lizzy ran into her father's office with her fairy house. "You're never going to believe what I've found."

But Dr Griffiths was studying the butterfly he had captured. He was going to take it to the museum.

Lizzy ran upstairs to her room, followed by Mr Twitches. She slowly took the lid off the fairy house. Tinker Bell darted out. Mr Twitches lunged for her.

"Mr Twitches, no! Bad cat!" Lizzy grabbed Tinker Bell and put her in a birdcage, where the cat couldn't reach her. Then, she picked up the cat and headed for the door. "Don't worry, little fairy! Mr Twitches won't bother you as long as you're in there."

Vidia knew she had to rescue Tink, but she needed help. She rushed back to fairy camp.

"Tinker Bell's been captured by humans!" Vidia told them everything.

The fairies made a plan to rescue Tinker Bell right away. But outside, it had started raining hard.

Fawn looked at the falling drops. "We can't fly in the rain."

Clank and Bobble, two other tinker fairies, had an idea. "We're gonna build a boat."

At the Griffiths' house, Lizzy opened the birdcage. Tinker Bell cautiously stepped out, then she darted to the window.

"I'm not going to hurt you . . . I just want to be your friend."

Lizzy showed Tink her collection of fairy notes and drawings.

Tink realized that the little girl loved fairies. She tried to tell Lizzy what fairies were really like, but all Lizzy could hear was a jingling sound, like the ringing of a bell.

"So that's how fairies speak. . . . So what do you think of my fairies. . . . Oh! And my fairy house!"

Tink flew over to the fairy house and began to fix the jammed door.

"Well, you're quite the little tinker, aren't you?"

Tinker Bell pointed to herself and then rang the little house's bell.

Lizzy realized the fairy was trying to tell her something. "Tinker Bell! Oh, what a lovely name."

Just then, Dr Griffiths came upstairs. When he heard the sound of
Lizzy's voice, he opened her bedroom door. Tinker Bell quickly hid.

"Lizzy, who are you talking to?"

Lizzy held up one of her fairy drawings. "My fairy!"

Dr Griffiths frowned. He didn't want Lizzy to waste her time
dreaming about fairies. He handed her a small book. "Here is a blank
field journal. I'm sure you'll be able to fill it with your own scientific
research." Then he went back into the hallway to fix a leak in the
ceiling.

Tinker Bell came out of her hiding spot and landed on the window sill.

She wanted to go back to her friends.

Lizzy looked disappointed. "Oh, I really wish you'd stay." She opened the window.

But when Tink saw how hard it was raining, she looked sad.

"Can't you fly in the rain?"

Tinker Bell shook her head.

"You can stay with me until the rain stops!"

Tinker Bell agreed. They got to work on Lizzy's new journal.

Meanwhile, Tinker Bell's friends had finished building their boat. They set out down the flooded path through the meadow.

Fawn climbed to the top of the mast to get a better look at what lay ahead. Suddenly, she gasped. "Hey, guys! We're heading right for a waterfall!"

Silvermist, a water-talent fairy, had an idea. She leaned over the edge of the boat and put her fingers in the water. She concentrated hard, and soon the water level rose so that the drop over the falls wasn't as steep. The boat sailed over the roaring rapids and crashed into the grass on the shore.

Vidia looked around. None of the fairies were hurt, but the boat was destroyed. "Looks like we're walking from here."

Tinker Bell and Lizzy had finished working on Lizzy's journal.

Tinker Bell flew out the window to go back to fairy camp, but she stopped when she heard Lizzy's voice. "Father, look."

Lizzy was trying to show her father her fairy journal. "I made it especially for you, Father. It's just like your field journal – it's filled with lots of facts. . . ."

"I don't have time. I have to find some way to deal with all these leaks."

Tink looked in the direction of the fairy camp, where her friends were waiting. Then she looked back at the house. She knew what she had to do.

Lizzy sat on her bed flipping through her fairy journal. There were tears in her eyes.

Suddenly, a small shadow appeared over the journal. "Tinker Bell! You came back." Lizzy beamed when the fairy landed right in her hand. "Oh, Tinker Bell, Father has no time for the field journal."

Tinker Bell smiled. She wiped away Lizzy's tears. "I think I can fix that."

Meanwhile, Vidia got stuck in the mud while trying to help the other fairies cross a road. The fairies tried to pull her out, but it was no use.

Suddenly, the fairies were hit with a flash of light. A car was coming! Fawn began to panic. "Come on! Hurry!"

But Iridessa, a light-talent fairy, had an idea. She stuck her hand into the beam of light and bent it back toward the driver. He thought another vehicle was heading straight for him and he slammed on his brakes. The car skidded to a stop just inches from where Vidia was stuck.

The car door opened, and a big boot stepped out. The driver was confused. "Hello? Is somebody out there?"

Fawn noticed that the driver's shoelace was untied. "Grab this! Hurry!"

Vidia looked at her in disbelief. "Are you kidding me?"

But Fawn knew her plan would work. "Trust me. And hold on tight."

All the fairies grabbed the driver's shoelace. As he turned to get back in his car, they were pulled out of the mud!

Back at Lizzy's house, Tinker Bell set to work fixing the leaks in Dr Griffiths' office. She hoped that would give Dr Griffiths more time to spend with Lizzy.

Tinker Bell flew into the dark, musty attic, where she found two leaks in the roof. She searched through old crates and boxes until she found the parts she needed. Then she got to work.

Soon she had set up a system that sent the water coming into the house back out again. She had stopped the leaks!

On her way back to Lizzy's room, Tinker Bell flew past Dr Griffiths' office. There, she spotted the butterfly Lizzy and her father had seen in the garden. It was trapped in a jar on Dr Griffiths' desk.

Tinker Bell wanted to help it.

A little while later, Dr Griffiths noticed that the leaks had stopped. Then he saw that the jar on his desk was empty. He showed Lizzy the empty jar. "The butterfly is gone! Did you release it?"

Lizzy was as surprised as her father. "No. . . "

"Well, I didn't do it, and since there is no one else in the house, there is only one logical explanation. It must have been you."

"I didn't do it, Father."

Dr Griffiths didn't believe his daughter. "I'm very disappointed in you." He sent Lizzy to her room.

Outside, Tinker Bell's friends were almost to the house.

Suddenly, Vidia stopped everyone. "Tinker Bell getting trapped is all my fault. I slammed that door on Tinker Bell to teach her a lesson. And now I've put her and all of us in danger. I am so sorry."

Rosetta looked at Vidia. "Oh, honey, this is not your fault. We all know that Tink can get into plenty of trouble all by herself."

Vidia was shocked. "I don't know what to say."

Rosetta held out her hand. The other fairies put their hands over hers. "How about faith . . . trust . . ."

Vidia clasped hands with the others. "And pixie dust!"

Tinker Bell followed Lizzy back to her room. "I'm so sorry, Lizzy."

Lizzy looked at Tink. "I'm so glad you're here. I wish I were a fairy."

Tinker Bell smiled. She had an idea.

She motioned for Lizzy to spread her arms wide and close her eyes. Then Tink flew above Lizzy's head and sprinkled her with pixie dust.

Suddenly, Lizzy's pigtails began to float. Next, her whole body lifted up off the floor. Lizzy grabbed on to the bedpost. She didn't know what was happening!

Tinker Bell smiled. She showed Lizzy how to move her arms and legs. After a short lesson, Lizzy was flying!

"Look at me! Wheeee, I'm a fairy!"

Downstairs, the fairy rescue team had finally arrived! Vidia and the rest of Tinker Bell's friends cautiously entered the Griffiths' kitchen.

"Okay, Tinker Bell is upstairs. The little girl has her in a cage. There's also a large human in the house who doesn't like creatures with wings. He pins them up in display cases."

Fawn looked worried. "Great! Anything else?"

"Oh, yes. The cat."

Suddenly, Mr Twitches appeared in the kitchen doorway. He pounced just as the fairies took off. They climbed onto a nearby shelf, spilling pixie dust on a set of dishes.

The cups, plates and saucers all began to hover in the air.

Vidia had an idea. She jumped from plate to plate, using the dishes as a bridge. The other fairies followed – but so did Mr Twitches.

Rosetta noticed that Vidia had almost crossed the kitchen. "You get to Tink, and we'll take care of the cat!"

"Got it!" Vidia made her way to the staircase and began to climb it one step at a time.

While the fairies were battling Mr Twitches, Dr Griffiths went to Lizzy's room. He'd heard lots of bumps and crashes. "What's going on in here?"

"Nothing."

Dr Griffiths looked around. "Look at this room! It looks like a cyclone hit it. How did you get footprints on the ceiling?"

Lizzy looked nervously at her father. "I was flying. My fairy showed me how."

"Oh, for goodness sake! You've got to stop this nonsense!"

Tinker Bell was furious. She flew out of her hiding spot, right into Dr Griffiths' face.

Dr Griffiths stumbled backward in shock. "It's . . . it's . . . extraordinary. This is going to be the discovery of the century!"

Vidia entered the room just as Dr Griffiths grabbed a jar and lowered it toward Tinker Bell. "Tink! Watch out!"

Vidia zoomed over and knocked Tink out of the way. Tinker Bell was safe! But the jar came down over Vidia instead. She was trapped!

Dr Griffiths ran out of the room with the jar in his hand. "I must get this to the museum right away!"

"Father, no!" Lizzy tried to stop him, but he wouldn't listen. He hopped in his car and drove off.

Suddenly, Tink and Lizzy heard Mr Twitches meowing. He walked into the room with Tinker Bell's friends on his back. Rosetta had used catnip to tame him.

Tinker Bell was glad to see her friends. "Lizzy's father trapped Vidia in a jar while she was saving me. We have to hurry and rescue her!"

Fawn told Tink that it was still raining. "How are we going to get there?"

Tinker Bell thought for a moment. "Maybe we can't fly, but I think I know somebody who can."

A few minutes later, Lizzy stood in the middle of the kitchen wearing a rain slicker and hat.

Tink turned to her friends. "All right fairies, we need all the pixie dust we can get. This girl's got a long journey ahead of her."

The fairies showered Lizzy with pixie dust from head to foot. When they were done, Lizzy began to lift up off the floor.

Tinker Bell settled on the collar of Lizzy's coat. "All aboard!"

The other fairies flew into Lizzy's pockets. Then Lizzy flew through the kitchen door and up, up, up into the sky. "I'm flying!"

The sky grew dark and the rain stopped as Lizzy soared through the clouds.

Soon the group spotted the lights of London twinkling below.

As Lizzy descended toward the city, she spotted her father's car.

"There he is! Tinker Bell, I can't keep up. He's going too fast!"

Tinker Bell took off toward the car and was soon flying right next to it. Inside, she could see Vidia in the jar.

Vidia was surprised to see Tinker Bell. "Tink!"

Tinker Bell nodded. Then, she dove beneath the car.

"Tinker Bell, no!"

Flying upside down, Tink studied the engine. It was full of dangerous, whirring parts. She tried her best to stay away from them as she tugged on pipes and wires. The engine began to spark and sputter, and soon, the car came to a stop.

Dr Griffiths banged on the steering wheel. "No, no, no, no, no, no!" He grabbed the jar with Vidia inside and began to run the rest of the way to the museum.

Lizzy and Tinker Bell were right on his heels. "Father!"

Dr Griffiths stopped. He turned around slowly to see Lizzy flying toward him. "Lizzy . . . you're . . . flying!"

Lizzy smiled. "Yes, I am! My friends showed me how."

Tinker Bell flew up next to Lizzy, and the other fairies flew out of her pockets. Dr Griffiths was in shock. "I . . . I don't understand."

"You don't have to understand. You just have to believe."

"I do believe. I do believe." Dr Griffiths opened his arms, and Lizzy rushed into them. "Oh, Lizzy, I'm so sorry. I'll never doubt you again."

Dr Griffiths let go of Lizzy. He handed her the jar.

Lizzy smiled as she unscrewed the lid and watched Vidia fly out.

"Vidia!" Tinker Bell wrapped her in a hug. The other fairies surrounded them, glowing bright with joy.

Then the fairies flew over to Lizzy and Dr Griffiths and sprinkled them both with pixie dust. They rose slowly into the air.

Lizzy watched her father begin to fly. "You're doing it, Father!"

"Why, I . . . I think I'm getting the hang of it. Yes. Why, I'm flying!"

Together, they rose over the city streets and flew home.

The next day, the fairies joined Lizzy and Dr Griffiths for a tea party in the meadow. Tinker Bell and Vidia sipped tea together. The other fairies flew in with a crown of flowers for Lizzy.

"Isn't this pleasant, Father?"

Dr Griffiths beamed as a firefly named Blaze dropped three lumps of sugar into his teacup. "I can't imagine anything better."

When they had finished their tea and snacks, everyone sat back and listened as Dr Griffiths read from Lizzy's fairy journal.

Terence flew up next to Tinker Bell. "Well, Tink, you found something to fix after all."

Tinker Bell looked at Lizzy and her father snuggled close together and smiled. "Yeah, I guess I did."